BOOK 1

Josie and the Fourth Grade Bike Brigade

by **A.B.K. Bruno**

illustrated by **Janet Pedersen**

Dedicated to the
children of P.S. 321
Brooklyn, NY

Printed in the United States.

10 9 8 7 6 5 4 3 2 1

Green Writers Press is a Vermont-based publisher whose mission is to spread a
message of hope and renewal through the words and images we publish.
Throughout we will adhere to our commitment to preserving and protecting the
natural resources of the earth. To that end, a percentage of our proceeds will be
donated to the environmental activist group, 350.org. We will also give a
percentage of our profits from this project directly to Vermont-based
environmental organizations. Green Writers Press gratefully acknowledges
support from individual donors, friends, and readers to help support the
environment and our publishing initiative.
Giving Voice to Writers Who Will Make the World a Better Place
Green Writers Press | Brattleboro, Vermont
www.greenwriterspress.com
www.josiegoesgreen.com

isbn: 978-09960872-2-3

cover & book design
Janet Pedersen

GREEN
WRITERS
press

CONTENTS

—1—

Grandma and the Whale

"Wake up Josie, wake up!" Someone was shaking me. I looked at the clock next to my bed. It said 6:02 a.m. For a second I thought it was a school day back home in Brooklyn, and my mom was waking me up. Then I saw my Grandma Carmen, and I remembered that it was summer and I was in Ecuador. Why in the world was she waking me so early? Before I could complain, Grandma was pulling the covers off my big brother Damien, trying to get him up. He was 12 and getting to be a real sleepyhead.

"Get up. Now!" yelled Grandma. "The Rescue Center called on the radio. There's a baby humpback whale stranded on the beach. We need to help get it back in the water."

Grandma doesn't usually get so excited. My tiredness vanished. This was a big deal. Now even Damien jumped out of bed.

My grandma is a marine biologist, speaks perfect English, Spanish and French, can beat Damien at arm wrestling and is simply the coolest grandma in the world. I knew she was in charge of volunteers at the Whale Rescue Center. But I'd been coming to her home in Ecuador every summer of my life – that's nine summers, by the way – and this was the first time I'd heard of a real whale emergency.

Damien and I practically flew into the car.

○ ○ ○

Grandma was driving fast. Suddenly there were policemen waving us over to the side of the road. An officer approached our car. I thought we were going to get a ticket. But that wasn't the problem.

"*Lo siento*," he said. "The road is closed for construction. You'll have to go around." He was speaking slowly enough for me to understand his Spanish.

But you didn't need to understand Spanish to know there was no time to go around the long way. You could see that from Grandma's face. She had told us that a baby whale can't live very long out of water.

Grandma turned the car around and grabbed the phone. Her friend Juana must have been on her speed dial because the next thing I knew Grandma was shouting at her a mile a minute.

"Juana, necesito tres bicicletas ahora mismo." "I need three bicycles right away. We have to get to the beach by the back road. A baby whale is stranded, probably since last night."

Grandma hung up without even waiting for an answer. She turned the car around and drove to Juana's house. Juana was waiting with four bicycles – three for us and one for her. Without a word we all jumped out of the car and onto the bikes and were pedaling like mad.

The police waved us through this

time. Pretty soon we were at the beach, huffing and puffing.

At first I couldn't see the whale, because it was in the shallow water and a crowd was gathered around it. Grandma was already running down to the whale and we ran behind her.

I had never seen a whale up close. This "baby" was a giant. Its skin was smooth in some parts and full of bumps and lumps in other parts. Its big gray eye looked right at me. Everyone there was getting ready to push.

"OK, everyone," Grandma shouted. "We have to keep her wet until the tide comes in. Then there'll be enough water for us to turn her and push her out."

"Carmen, it's already coming in. High

tide is in 3 hours," someone was saying.

"Then we'll keep her wet for three hours," replied Grandma.

Suddenly half the crowd was running to their cars and bikes and shouting into their cell phones calling for buckets, sheets, towels and hoses.

The other half of the crowd stayed with the whale. There were people standing in the water on either side of the whale, throwing water on her to keep her skin wet. When their arms got tired, Damien and I took our turns. My legs even bumped up against the whale's side. It was much rougher than I expected, and hurt my skin.

Finally, after about two hours, we noticed that the whale was sort of floating.

"OK everyone." Grandma Carmen was still in charge. "Let's try to turn this baby."

"*Uno, dos, y tres,*" yelled Grandma. But the whale barely budged.

"C'mon, everybody at once!"

At least 30 people crowded around the whale and we tried to turn her. We knocked into each other and fell down, splashing into the water. Little by little we got the whale's head facing out to sea.

But she didn't move.

We pushed.

She still didn't move.

We pushed harder.

Nothing happened.

Then we heard it. A sound that was like a train grumbling and then a door squeaking.

"What the..."

"It's her mother!" cried Grandma.

We looked up. There was another whale in the deep water. It was the mother whale, and she was talking.

Just then, the baby whale moved her tail. It knocked me down.

"Careful, everyone. Out of the way!"

Our baby whale flicked her tail a couple of times more, and suddenly she was in the deep water, swimming to her

mother. She glided away smoothly, as if nothing had happened.

And just like that, it was over.

"We did it, we did it!" I yelled. Now everyone was shouting and slapping hands and slapping backs.

"Hooray for Carmen!" someone shouted.

"Hooray for all of you," said Grandma.

"Hooray for Juana's bicycles," said Damien quietly.

"True," I thought.

We were all wet anyway so we decided to take a swim. Pretty soon we just sat down on the sand. "Josie, look at this beautiful beach." My grandmother spread her arms wide as she spoke. I looked at the miles and miles of sand, going on forever. The sun was making the sand sparkle as though someone had put glitter in it.

"When I was your age," said Grandma, "my grandma took me here to swim. I think these beaches are the most beautiful in the world."

"Did it always look like this?" I asked.

"Well, the beach is the same. But the road is new. When I was your age there were no cars here, and it was even more beautiful without them." She pointed to the road behind us where we had left the bikes. As I looked, I saw a blue car exactly like my friend Lizzy's. She and Matt are my best friends. I picked up some shells and tucked them in my pocket to give to Matt and Lizzy on the first day of school.

School! Holy Moly, it would be starting soon. I always think about what I should wear on my first day. Definitely the brown and red sneakers that Grandma bought me in town. Those new sneakers are the coolest.

Grandma broke into my thoughts. "Let's get some ice cream," she said. It was still morning. But she knows that ice cream's important. *Very* important.

2

Fortunately, Unfortunately

On the first day of school I was too excited to sleep, so at exactly 6:47 I wrote my grandma an email, and she answered right back.

To: garciacarmen86@whalemail.com
From: Josieposie99@bearmail.com
Subject: Hola

Hola, Grandma. I'm back in Brooklyn, it's early morning, and guess what? I'm starting fourth grade TODAY. I can't wait to tell everyone about the whale!!! I forgot to ask you: did the whale ever come back? Matt and

Lizzy will want to know.

I love you more than a thousand oceans plus infinity.

Josie

====================

To: Josieposie99@bearmail.com
From: garciacarmen86@whalemail.com
Subject: Re: Hola

Querida Josie,

Buenos días. Have a great first day at school. Tell Matt and Lizzy I haven't seen the whale again, which is a good thing.

I love you more than every whale in the world times 20 infinities.

Grandma

"Get going or you'll be late," my mom yelled. I definitely didn't want to be late on my first day. There was no time to worry about my first day clothes after all. I threw on a shirt, gobbled some toast, brushed my teeth, slipped on my lucky brown and red sneakers and ran out the door. Actually, they're not just my "lucky" sneakers, they're my only sneakers.

First my mom started the car, and then she started the car game. It's a game we always play when we're in the car. It helps me relax if I'm nervous about something, like the first day of school.

Mom: "Unfortunately, vacation is over."

Me: "Fortunately, I can't wait to go to school and see my friends."

Mom: "Unfortunately, it's going to be much harder this year now that you're in 4th grade."

Me: "Fortunately, I probably won't get homework on the first day."

Mom: "Unfortunately, you have to clean your room."

Me: "Fortunately, I'm not coming home after school."

Mom: "Unfortunately, that means you'll miss ice cream."

Me: "Fortunately, I have some chocolate ice cream right here in my backpack."

Mom: "Unfortunately it melted."

If you try the Fortunately-Unfortunately Car Game, you probably will find that it usually ends with melting ice cream.

Ice cream reminded me of my grandma, the whale and the beach.

As we pulled up to the school, a thought occurred to me. "Mom," I asked, "what did Parkside look like before the roads were built?"

"I don't know, Josie," she replied, "but we can talk about it later. Have a great first day of 4th Grade."

"Thanks, Mom."

I hopped out. I saw Matt and Lizzy standing by the front door of school and I ran over to them. We all threw our arms around each other. It was so great to be together again.

Lizzy started talking fast. "Josie, thank you for all the emails. You're the best.

Ecuador sounds incredible. Next year, can I come with you?"

"Josie, what class are you in?" Matt asked.

"Don't you remember? You dodo bird. Lizzy and I are in 402."

"Oh! I'm in 402, too. Same class!" Matt loves saying obvious things.

In the playground, we found a woman holding a sign that said 402. Underneath that, it said "Ms. Sheyla."

"Do you think the woman holding the sign is Ms. Sheyla?" asked Matt.

"Duh," said Lizzy.

I got in line behind the 402 sign. I tried to stand on my toes and look at the rest of my class, but Lizzy tugged on my sleeve. "Eddie's at the back of the line," she whispered. Lizzy knows me pretty well. I looked at the back of the line. Eddie was the cutest boy in the fourth grade.

In the classroom, I dragged Matt and Lizzy to the front of the room to sit next to me. We were sitting on the floor, and Eddie was right across from me. My feet seemed to stick way out and take up the whole room. Right then, I silently thanked my grandma for the brown and red sneakers. Ooh, they looked good.

3

Frozey

A few days later, we were writing in our notebooks, when Ms. Sheyla flicked off the lights to get our attention.

"Class," she said, "this Friday we are going on a trip to the Bronx Zoo."

The class cheered, except for David, my enemy since first grade. He never got excited about anything except evil ideas, like the time he put a dead spider in my friend Elsa's desk and made her scream in the middle of class. I can't stand David.

Neither can Matt. Just then, he

pretended to yank on David's hair. I started laughing and Ms. Sheyla looked up, annoyed. "Yes, Josie?" I tried to stop laughing, but I'm really bad at stopping once I start.

Luckily Ms. Sheyla decided to ignore me. "As I was saying," she continued, "this Friday we will go to the zoo. We will be looking at a new exhibit of polar bears. I expect everyone to be on their best behavior for this trip." She looked straight at David. Teachers like Ms. Sheyla are smart, and she had already figured out that if anyone would make trouble on a field trip, it was David.

Matt raised his hand, and Ms. Sheyla called on him. "I think anyone who misbehaves should be fed to the polar bears," he announced. I'm not sure, but I think Ms. Sheyla was trying not to smile.

○ ○ ○

Friday morning, the day of our trip to the zoo, I bounded out of bed as soon as the alarm rang. We had to get to school early and take a train to the zoo. Ms. Sheyla made us all choose buddies. Darn it, Isa was standing right next to Eddie and got to be partners with him. So I grabbed Lizzy's hand and pulled her near Eddie and Isa. Eddie smiled at me and I blushed.

On the train, we tried to balance while singing "Surfin' Safari" every time our train stopped. David tried to surf on one foot, but he fell. Then he rolled and ended up with his legs on someone's lap.

Lizzy looked at me because she knew I would start laughing. Whenever I see someone fall, I can't help laughing. I try to wait to make sure they're not hurt, but sometimes I laugh first. Luckily, most of the other kids were laughing too, though not as hard as me.

Finally, we got to the zoo. A man with a uniform greeted us at the entrance. "I'm Ranger Willy," he said, smiling. He led us to the polar bears. "Everyone be good today, because these polar bears get VERY hungry." I remembered what Matt said about kids who misbehaved being fed to the bears, and I looked at Ms. Sheyla. Did she try to hide a smile again?

Ranger Willy told us more about the polar bears. "Polar bears need about 10-20 pounds of food per day," said the ranger. "In the wild they eat mostly seal meat, but here in the zoo we feed them fish. These polar bears come from Alaska. Their names are Freezy – that's the huge female over there – and Frozey – that's the even huger male one over there."

The polar bears were playing in their pool, jumping off the ice and swimming back and forth. Their black noses stuck out of the water, and their legs went flat behind them when they swam. Then somehow they would jump out and show their giant claws. When they walked their shoulders looked powerful. I wanted to keep listening to Ranger Willy, but it was hard because it was so much fun to watch the bears. How could animals that big be so playful?

"Polar bears need very cold places to live," said the Ranger. "Life is getting harder for polar bears in the wild because the earth is getting warmer and the ice where they hunt is melting."

Then I completely lost track of what he was saying because one of the polar bears was looking at me. It was Frozey. He was swimming back and forth in the water between the ice. Every time he came toward us, he looked right at me. It was like he could see straight into my head. I met his eyes and whispered "hello" to him. He looked at me without moving his head, but I think he was trying to say

"hello" back. My eyes started tearing from trying not to blink, but I kept staring into his deep black eyes.

The spell was broken by Freezy, who jumped in the water and roared, with her teeth bared. The class screamed, and I don't blame them. It was pretty scary.

David glanced at Ms. Sheyla and stopped his fooling around.

When the bears settled down, I tried to listen to Ranger Willy again. "As I was saying," he said, "life is getting harder for polar bears because the earth is getting warmer and the ice is melting. They are running out of places with enough ice for them to live in."

Isa raised her hand. "Do you have a question, young lady?" asked Ranger Willy.

"Why is the earth getting warmer? Is that because the sun is growing?" she asked. To be honest, I couldn't figure out why the earth would be getting warmer either, but Isa is never afraid to ask questions.

"No," said Ranger Willy, "the earth is

getting warmer because of something called global warming. Global warming is making the whole earth get a little hotter all the time. That means that the ice where polar bears live is gradually melting."

"Why is global warming happening?" Isa asked. She was looking at Freezy and Frozey and she seemed upset. I was a little scared too. If the polar bears' ice was melting, how long would it take for *everything* to melt?

"There are lots of reasons for global warming. We have to use some really big words to talk about them. Are you ready for some big words?"

"We're ready," we yelled.

"Mostly it's because of pollution from electricity generation, deforestation and cars."

"What's pollution?" asked Isa.

"What's generation?" asked Lizzy.

"What's deforestation?" asked David.

"What's a car?" asked Matt. Lizzy pretended to punch him.

Ranger Willy sighed and said, "I'll have to let Ms. Sheyla cover that back in class because we have to move on to the seals. It's their feeding time, and that's always fun to watch."

The seals were pretty cool. But I couldn't stop thinking about Frozey and the global warming that was melting the ice in Alaska.

"Josie, what are you thinking?" It was Matt of course. He knows me pretty well, too. He could tell I was up to something.

"We have to do something, Matt. We have to help the polar bears."

"How?"

"Ranger Willy said their ice is melting."

"Yeah, he said the globe is warming."

"Right! Global warming. That's what we have to stop."

"Uh-oh," said Matt.

"What do you mean, Uh-oh?" I asked.

"I mean here we go again. In a good way, Josie."

"That's a good uh-oh?"

"Exactly."

"Then you'll help me." I said, satisfied.

Matt didn't answer. But he always helps me in the end.

4

See-Oh-Too

The next day Ms. Sheyla continued the lesson on global warming.

"Global warming is caused by a certain kind of air pollution," she began. Who knows what pollution is?"

"I know," yelled David. "Farts! That's air pollution!" The whole class laughed. Eddie laughed so hard he fell off his chair.

"No, David," said Ms. Sheyla. "Farts are natural. Anyone else?"

Lizzy's hand shot into the air. Lizzy

should be in sixth grade or something, she knows so much. "Pollution is when something harmful goes into the air, water or ground that doesn't belong there," she said.

"I couldn't have said it better myself," said Ms. Sheyla.

The lesson went on, but I couldn't pay attention. I was starting to wonder if global warming was going to affect the beach near Grandma's. Or even Parkside.

○   ○   ○

After school that day, Lizzy and I went to the library and read about climate change. That's another way of saying global warming.

Lizzy said, "Look here, Josie. It says that the biggest cause of climate change is an invisible gas called carbon dioxide. CO_2 for short."

"But CO_2 is natural, Lizzy."

"I guess CO_2 is not a bad thing. But too much CO_2 is really, really bad." As I said, Lizzy is probably the smartest person I know. Then we had fun figuring out all the ways we could write CO_2:

See-oh-too

C-O-2

Sea-O-Two

Say-Oh-Dos

(That's how my grandma would say it in Spanish.)

Lizzy even started singing the National Anthem, "Oh Say Can You See Oh Two," until the librarian told us to quiet down.

Suddenly Lizzy said, "Look at this Josie, Ranger Willy is right. Driving cars is one of the main causes of climate change because cars burn gasoline and that creates CO2."

Cars! The same cars that Grandma thought ruined her beach. The same cars that I loved to play Fortunately-Unfortunately in. The same cars that cause the traffic jams that my father hates so much.

Fixing this problem wasn't going to be easy. We drive almost every day! But we had to start somewhere. And I knew where.

5

The Fourth Grade
Bike Brigade

To: garciacarmen86@whalemail.com
From: Josieposie99@bearmail.com
Subject: Climate Change

Hola Abuelita,

We took a field trip and saw polar bears.
They weren't as big as the whale, but they
were still enormous. And beautiful. We also
learned about global warming. It's pretty
scary. It's already pretty hot in Ecuador. I
hope you're not going to melt.

Lizzy thinks that one way we can help is by driving less. I was thinking about the whale rescue. When we couldn't drive, we biked. I'm thinking about starting to bike to school every day.

What do you think about that?

Love you more than a million billion infinities times the weight of the biggest whale in the world.

Josie

P.S. I learned that climate change and global warming are the same thing.

To: Josieposie99@bearmail.com
From: garciacarmen86@whalemail.com
Subject: Climate Change

Josie

We marine biologists know all about global warming because it makes the ocean warmer, too. It happens very slowly, so I won't melt. But it needs to be stopped.

Biking to school is a perfect idea! I would love to see the whole world get out of their cars and onto their bikes, just like we did the morning of the whale rescue. Start with you and your friends, and then see what happens.

Love you more than all the grains of sand on the beach times all the stars in the sky,

Tu Abuelita

○ ○ ○

"Mom, Dad, where's my bike?" I yelled when I woke up the next morning.

"Honey, where's her bike?" asked my dad.

"I don't know, why are you asking me?" said Mom.

"Well, you're a better looker than me."

"You mean I'm better looking."

"That too," said my dad.

It's true. My mom can always find things when the rest of us can't. My dad tries to butter her up to get her to look for things. But this was no time for his jokes.

"Dad! I can't be late today." I had told my parents about global warming and my plan already, so I thought they would understand how serious this was.

"Josie, I brought it outside already." That was Damien speaking. He had also gotten the bike ready by pumping up the tires.

"Wow, D. Thanks!" I said.

"Whatever," he grumbled. But if Mr. Sleepyhead was helping this early in the morning when he could have slept an extra five minutes instead, he knew it was important too.

And it was important. As important as doing my homework. As important as sitting near Eddie. Maybe as important as ice cream.

It was the first day of Operation Save the Polar Bears, also known as the

Fourth Grade Bike Brigade. If cars were causing global warming, then we could help by driving less. Lizzy and I had figured it all out at the library, and even Grandma agreed it was a good idea.

The plan was for Matt, Lizzy and me to meet up and then all ride together. I live farther from school than Matt, so I left first. I've ridden to his house lots of times. But this felt different, because I was riding to school. When I got to Matt's house and saw his bike, I could have kissed him, even though he's not Eddie. He had attached a pole to the back of his bike and tied an adorable stuffed polar bear to the pole. "Pole-Our Bear. Get it?" said Matt.

I didn't get it, but that's OK, Matt has his own style.

The next stop was Lizzy's. Lizzy's bike is bright purple, and her long hair is bright orange. She looked great. "Matt," she said. "You didn't tell us you were tying a bear to your bike. Why do you keep all the best ideas secret?"

Before Matt could answer, Lizzy showed us a surprise of her own. She turned her back to us, and we saw it. Her shirt said,

SAVE THE POLAR BEARS
BIKE TO SCHOOL

"That's why we love you, Lizzy," I said. Lizzy turned around, and Matt gave the thumbs up sign. Then he gave two thumbs up. That was not smart, because he had to let go of the handlebars. Matt fell over.

Did I mention my little problem? I can't help laughing when people fall down. Well, Matt wasn't hurt, and luckily, he thought it was funny, too.

"Let's go! For Freezy and Frozey," said Lizzy.

Now imagine how good we looked. Lizzy in front, her orange hair coming out from under her helmet. Matt behind us with the polar bear floating above him. And me, well, I had my brown and red sneakers on the pedals.

Our friends waved and yelled out their windows as they went by in their

cars. When we pulled up, lots of kids crowded around asking questions.

"Did your parents let you do this?"

"Did you get out of breath?"

"What's the polar bear doing?"

"Who won the race?"

We told everyone why we were biking. And then I heard the question I had been really been hoping for.

"Can I ride with you tomorrow?"

Guess what? It was Eddie who asked first. By the end of the day, most of the class was ready to join the Fourth Grade Bike Brigade.

The Captains

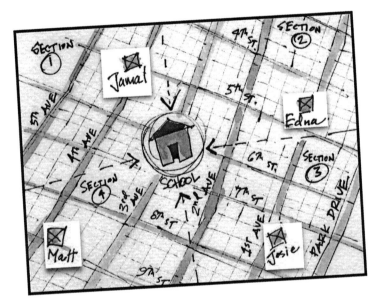

Now that so many people wanted to bike with us, we needed to figure out how to all meet in the morning. So after school, Lizzy and Matt went to the office and got an address list that showed where all the kids lived. Then they brought it to my house, and we looked at it next to my dad's map of the neighborhood. We put a little sticker next to every kid's building. The stickers surrounded the school on the map.

"We can't all ride together," said Lizzy, looking at the list and the map. "We're coming from different directions."

Matt seemed deep in thought. Finally, he said, "We can find four captains, one for each part of the neighborhood." Lizzy and I smiled at each other. Matt didn't usually have good plans. Or any plans. But this was a great plan. We split the neighborhood into four sections. That was enough for one day.

I really wanted to ask Eddie to be a captain. He lived on 5th Street, in Section 1. Unfortunately, Eddie was late to school a lot. Fortunately, Jamal also lived on 5th Street and he was always on time. And he had a really nice bicycle, with curvy handlebars and a bell. I decided to ask Jamal to be our captain for Section 1.

"Jamal," I said to him after school on Monday, "How would you like to be the captain of Section 1 for the Fourth Grade Bike Brigade?"

"Whoa. Slow down there, Josie," said Jamal. "What are you talking about?"

"Remember the polar bears we saw at the zoo?"

"Freezy and Frozey. I'll never forget them. Man those guys were big! Did you see their claws?"

"Well, remember that the ranger told us that polar bears are in trouble because of global warming."

"Yeah," Jamal said slowly.

"Well, part of the problem is that we're polluting the air by driving. So, a bunch of us are going to ride our bikes instead," I explained.

"Riding is cool," said Jamal.

I explained how the Fourth Grade Bike Brigade would work. "Each section of our neighborhood will have a captain. That would be you," I smiled my best smile. "You'll get all the kids in your section to ride to school. Tell them why it's important, and find out who needs a bicycle."

"I don't know, Josie. It sounds like a lot of work, and my parents make me do ALL my homework every single day."

"Jamal," I said, "before you decide, let's go visit the ice cream truck."

One chocolate cone with sprinkles later, Jamal was my first captain. I knew ice cream would do the trick.

○   ○   ○

Jamal's friend Edna lived on 1st Avenue, and she was perfect for a captain, plus she was a great artist. After Jamal and I told her why everyone

ANNOUNCING:

The Fourth Grade
Bike Brigade

<u>Save the Polar Bears!</u>
<u>Stop Global Warming!</u>
For More information contact:
Josie, Matt, Jamal or Edna.

should ride to school, Edna agreed to become a captain. She also made a beautiful poster and hung it up at school.

We also made flyers with the same information and gave them out to everyone.

Pretty soon, kids were coming up to me all day and calling me all night.

"Josie, I want to join but I don't have a helmet."

"Josie, I live on 2nd St., who's my captain?"

"Josie, can you explain to my parents why I need a new bike?"

My parents were getting mad because the phone was always ringing. But it was worth it because every day a few more kids joined.

Ten Gallons a Day

One month after our trip to the zoo, we had almost the entire Fourth Grade riding to school. We even got some of the teachers involved.

The science teacher, Ms. Kelly, showed us how to figure out how much gas we were saving. First we looked at a map and figured out how far away each of us drove to get to school. Some kids lived close, some lived far, and some took a bus. But Ms. Kelly explained we could take an average distance. We guessed that each family drove an average of a half mile to school. But then the parents had to drive back home, so that's about one mile. And they did it again to pick up their kids. So we figured it was about two

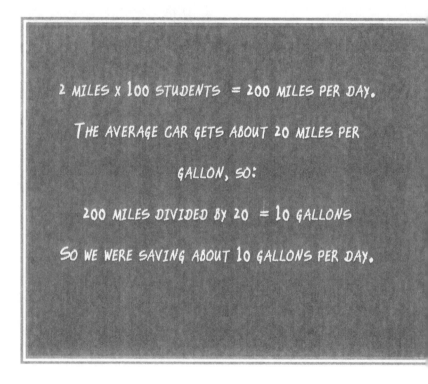

2 MILES x 100 STUDENTS = 200 MILES PER DAY.

THE AVERAGE CAR GETS ABOUT 20 MILES PER

GALLON, SO:

200 MILES DIVIDED BY 20 = 10 GALLONS

SO WE WERE SAVING ABOUT 10 GALLONS PER DAY.

miles a day per family. There were 150 kids in the Fourth Grade, and about 100 of them were riding to school.

"That's a lot of gasoline," I thought. Enough to fill up at the gas station 200

1 DAY = 10 GALLONS

1 WEEK = 50 GALLONS (THERE ARE FIVE DAYS IN A SCHOOL WEEK)

1 MONTH = 200 GALLONS (THERE ARE AT LEAST FOUR WEEKS IN A MONTH)

10 MONTHS = 2,000 GALLONS (THERE ARE 10 MONTHS IN THE SCHOOL YEAR)

times. Enough to fill 2,000 large milk containers. Grandma was going to be proud. I rushed home from school to send her an email.

To: Garciacarmen86@whalemail.com
From: Josieposie99@bearmail.com
Subject: It's working!

You're never going to believe it. Almost all the kids in fourth grade are riding bikes to school, just like we did for the whale rescue. My next plan is for the whole country to do it.

Love you more than 2,000 gallons (that's how much gasoline Ms. Kelly says we're saving).

Josie
To: Josieposie99@bearmail.com

From: Garciacarmen86@whalemail.com

Subject: Re: It's working!

Congratulations! I am so proud of you, preciosa. As for the whole country, well, let's break our big problems into little ones and solve them one at a time.

Love you more than the deepest well, times a few million infinities,

Abuelita Carmen

○ ○ ○

But after I sent that email to grandma, the problems started. On Tuesday, Leon forgot to lock up his bike and it got stolen. Lizzy, Matt and I spent all evening calling kids to see if someone had an extra bike they could lend him. Luckily, Rafael's aunt and uncle run a bike shop, and they promised to find him a cheap one.

On Wednesday, it rained and no one wanted to ride. I spent all evening calling my friends to tell them to remember to ride again on Thursday if it stopped raining.

On Thursday, Joey got a flat tire and was late for school. His teacher got mad.

On Friday,

something pretty bad happened. We were riding to school when suddenly a car started honking really loudly. It scared Matt, who was in the back of our brigade, and he swerved and hit the mirror of a parked car. The owner of the car was mad.

"Do you see what you've done?" he shouted to Matt.

"I seem to have hit the mirror," said Matt. But it was a bad time for one of his jokes.

The owner got madder and said Matt would have to pay for a new mirror. Now we were holding up traffic, and the cars were honking more. When we finally got to school, it was a relief.

But not for long. As soon as I got to class, Ms. Sheyla told me I needed to see the principal. Our principal, Ms. Blaylock, is pretty nice. Still, it's usually not good news when you have to go see her.

8

The Principal's Office

When I got to Ms Blaylock's office, I saw that my dad was there too! Uh-oh, I thought, this is cereal. That's what my dad always says instead of serious. How can you have a serious conversation with someone who wants to have a cereal conversation? There was also another man there, looking very important in a fancy suit and a nametag.

"Josie," said Ms. Blaylock. "This is Mr. Ford from the Community Council." I tried to say "Nice to meet you," but I don't think any words came out. "There has been a complaint about the Fourth Grade Bike Brigade."

"We'll pay for the mirror that M--, that got broken," I said.

Ms. Blaylock raised her eyebrows in surprise. So she didn't know about the mirror. And I almost told on my best friend. Me and my big mouth.

"Some people have been complaining that the bikes are slowing down traffic and that someone could get hit by a car. Now, I hear that you are the leader of the Bike Brigade," Ms. Blaylock continued.

Until now I had been very proud of the Bike Brigade. But now I wasn't sure it was such a good thing to be the leader of it. "Well, Edna is the captain of the First Avenue group, and..."

"What I think Josie means, Ms. Blaylock," interrupted my dad, "is that she had the idea, but all the kids are doing it together."

The man I didn't know, Mr. Ford, spoke. "It doesn't matter who started it. The point is, we at Community Council 13 believe it's dangerous. We don't want anyone to get hurt. We suggest that group bike rides can take place in the park after school." His voice was kinder than I thought it would be. But he sounded very cereal, as my dad would say.

"That would ruin it," I managed to squeak out.

"Why?" asked Ms. Blaylock.

"Lots of reasons," I said.

"Tell them why, Josie," said my dad.

I really wanted to cry. I really wanted to leave. Then I thought of Frozey. It helped me remember why.

"Riding after school won't stop global warming."

Mr. Ford looked annoyed. "Of course not," he said. "Global warming is a global problem. We can't do anything about it in our little neighborhood."

I continued, "If we ride after school instead of to school it won't reduce the gas we use in cars. And if we don't use less gas, we can't stop global warming. And if we don't stop global warming, we can't save the polar bears."

All the grownups seemed really surprised, and there was a long silence.

During that silence I came to an important realization. I really needed to go to the bathroom. The next time I have to go to the principal's office I'm going to stop at the bathroom first.

Finally, Ms. Blaylock came to the rescue. "Well, the staff at P.S. 99 did not start the Fourth Grade Bike Brigade, and we cannot end it. We can only control what happens when the students get to school, not how they get here."

Then my dad spoke again. "Mr. Ford," he said, "it seems this is a subject for the families of the neighborhood, not just the school."

Mr. Ford did not look too happy, but agreed to discuss it at the next Community Meeting. Everyone stood up. That meant I could leave. I headed straight for the bathroom. Then I wondered what would happen at the big meeting.

9

The Meeting

To: Garciacarmen86@whalemail.com
From: Josieposie99@bearmail.com
Subject: Community Meeting

Things are going crazy here Grandma. Some grownups are complaining about the bike brigade. There's going to be a community meeting about it tomorrow night.

If they don't let us ride any more I don't know what we'll do. I might have to quit school. :--)

Love you more than a million gazillions,

-J

To: Josieposie99@bearmail.com
From: garciacarmen86@whalemail.com
Subject: Re: Community Meeting

Josie, be ready to speak at the Community Meeting. Tell them why the bike brigade is important. Tell them everything. Tell them even if you're nervous. You'll be great.

And remember, I love you way more than infinity infinities.

-Abuelita

The night before the community meeting, just after I finished reading my grandma's email, my brother yelled,

"Josie, pick up the phone!"

"Who is it, Damien?"

"He said his name is Eddie."

Whee! My stomach did a little cartwheel. Eddie never called me. Why was he calling now?

"Hello?" I said, flattening my hair as I spoke even though he couldn't see me.

"Josie, it's me, Eddie."

"I know," I said.

"Rafael and I were talking about the Community Meeting."

"Yeah."

"Well, remember how his uncle and aunt have a bike shop?"

"Yes, I remember."

"Right. Well, Rafael says that his uncle will come to the community meeting and talk about bike safety," Eddie said.

"That would be so awesome," I told

him. I hoped he could see the huge grin on my face over the phone.

"I'm telling everyone to go to the meeting to show how important the bike brigade is."

I wanted to say "I love you, Eddie!" But I knew that would be wrong. Instead I said thank you, hung up, and twirled with joy all the way to my room.

The next day was school as usual. The grownups acted as if the most important community meeting in the history of Parkside was no big deal. They expected me to pay attention in class! Silly grownups.

On the ride home, Matt got right to the point. "How nervous are you?"

"Matt," I answered. "I'm so nervous I

think going to Ms. Blaylock's office would be relaxing."

"Then don't forget to go the bathroom before the meeting."

The meeting took place at our school, P.S. 99. Even though it was at night, my whole family rode our bikes over there, wearing shiny vests, blinking lights and helmets. "The whole nine yards of safety," my dad called it.

"Moving fireworks," said Damien.

The auditorium was packed! There were signs all over. "Safety First," said one. "We Have a Right To Ride," said another. Mine said, "Save the Polar Bears."

"What do polar bears have to do with it?" asked David's mom.

"You'll find out," said my dad.

I sat with my whole family. Lizzy was next to me. Matt, Eddie and Isa were just across the aisle. But someone was missing. Rafael wasn't there. Neither was his uncle. I looked at Eddie, a big question mark on my face. He shrugged, but looked worried.

Mr. Ford started the meeting. He

explained that there would be two
presentations, one for the Bike Brigade
and one against it. Then everyone would
have three minutes to comment. Finally,
the Community Council would vote.

If they voted against the Brigade, we
were doomed.

First the man whose mirror was
broken by Matt spoke. He talked about

how he had to slow down every morning. He said the bikes made him late for work. And, of course, he told about the mirror. He didn't mention that it was someone honking who scared Matt and caused the accident.

Then it was my turn. I told them everything, just like my Grandma said to. About Ecuador. About Frozey. About global warming, and how cars are one of the causes. I even told them about the Fortunately-Unfortunately Car Game, and how I loved our car. But, I told them, we had to drive less. Everybody stood up and clapped when I finished. Boy, did that feel great.

The rest of the meeting was a blur. Grownups get really excited at these things. They were shouting and interrupting. Everyone who spoke thought that he or she was right and that everyone else was wrong.

Someone said that we kids were setting a good example, and everyone should ride.

Another person said that if someone got hit by a car it would be a tragedy.

Someone else said she was going to invent a car that doesn't use gasoline.

Then it was Ms. Kelly's turn. She was our science teacher and a real scientist. No one was interrupting now. Everyone was listening.

Ms. Kelly said, "Our kids alone cannot save the polar bears." Mr. Ford looked very pleased. "However,"

(That's scientist talk for "but") continued Ms. Kelly, "the kids are saving about 2,000 gallons of gasoline a year. There are many benefits to using less gasoline. Less pollution. Saving money. Easier parking. Healthy exercise."

And then she used her best scientist voice. "In my scientific opinion, bike riding is beneficial to public health and the environment." She sat back down.

The entire Fourth Grade Bike Brigade stood up, waving our signs and cheering.

Then Mr. Ford called on himself to speak. "2,000 gallons less of gas will not save the polar bears. It's nice that kids in Parkside want to save polar bears in the Arctic, but unfortunately, it's more complicated than that."

Fortunately, lots of people want to help us, I thought.

Mr. Ford continued, "Safety is the most important thing. Therefore as President of the Community Council, I recommend stopping the Fourth Grade Bike Brigade."

I almost felt sick. Lizzy held my hand. My mom whispered, "Don't worry."

Mr. Ford spoke again. "The Council will now vote on whether the Fourth Grade Bike Brigade will be allowed to continue riding bicycles to school every day."

I looked down at my brown and red sneakers. They reminded me of my grandma and her beach. That reminded me of Frozey, who used to live near a beach in Alaska, which reminded me of Matt's bicycle with the polar bear on the back. I glanced up and looked for him. His eyes were squeezed shut. So were Eddie's and Isa's. I shut mine, too.

"All in favor..." Mr. Ford began.

"Wait. Please. Wait." Everyone turned to look for the new voice.

It was Rafael. "I am Rafael Goldstein from 7th St. This is my Uncle Max," he said, introducing the man standing next to him. "He is an expert on bicycle safety."

"We're all ready to vote," said Mr. Ford. "There's no time for another person to speak."

"Please, Mr. Ford," said Rafael's dad. "He came all the way from the Bronx.

The only reason he's late is traffic. You know how bad it gets out there."

"Yes, yes, I do. Arrrrggghhh, I hate traffic," Mr. Ford growled. Then he went silent and his face went red, the way my dad's does when he gets stuck in traffic. The crowd started grumbling. Finally Mr. Ford sighed, "Okay, you have three minutes."

"Thank you, Mr. Chairman," said Rafael's uncle. Wow, he's polite, I thought. "I hear there is a disagreement here over children who are biking to school. I think everyone agrees it is good for kids to ride bicycles, but not at the expense of safety. I believe there is a solution." I sat up straight. I listened as hard as I could. What could be the solution?

"The solution is to paint bike lanes on

the streets that are used by the children. Cars cannot use those lanes, not even for double parking. And groups of bike riders must stay in those lanes. They must wear helmets and bright clothing."

His three minutes weren't up but everyone started talking. Pretty soon the auditorium was louder than a Fourth Grade Assembly. These grownups sure are rowdy!

The Community Council Members gathered on the stage. A few minutes later Mr. Ford said they would vote. But now there was a new thing to vote on. They were voting on whether or not to paint bike lanes in Parkside.

Moments later, the vote was done.

Everyone agreed to paint bike lanes! The crowd was whooping and clapping like crazy. Everyone was congratulating me and hitting me on the back. Ouch!

The Fourth Grade Bike Brigade would continue. Soon we would get the 5th grade to ride, too, and the 6th and the 7th. Then we'd get our parents to ride to work.

Lizzy must have read my mind. "Look what you started, Josie," she whispered to me. "And we're not done. If everyone does something, we'll stop global warming."

"It's 10:00," interrupted my mom. "Let's ride home. We'll pretend the bike lanes are already there."

"But Mom and Dad," said Damien,

"aren't you forgetting something? Don't polar bears remind you of frozen things?"

My brother knows that ice cream's important. *Very* important.

the end

Discussion Guide

1. When Josie is in the principal's office, Mr. Ford from the Community Council says that global warming is a huge problem and Josie and her friends can't stop it by biking to school. Josie knows that biking is not enough to stop climate change, but she remains determined to do it anyway. Why do you think it is so important to Josie not to give up, even though she can't completely solve the problem by herself?

2. At the community meeting, Mr. Ford asks the council to vote "yes" or "no" on the fourth grade bike brigade. Uncle Max comes up with a third answer: painting bike lanes. Uncle Max shows that sometimes we have to be more creative than just saying "yes" or "no." How can you use this kind of thinking to make good choices? Can you think of an example? (Hint: You are in a store and they ask if you want a paper or plastic bag. But is there a third option?)

3. Josie notices that people are driving a lot in her community, which contributes to global warming. After seeing this problem, Josie comes up with a solution: biking! Biking does no harm to the environment, and it can be really fun, especially when you do it with friends. What do you notice people in your neighborhood doing that is bad for the planet? Can you think of a better way to do it? How would you get others to join you?

IF YOU HAVE QUESTIONS ABOUT
CLIMATE CHANGE OR COMMUNITY
ACTION, PLEASE VISIT
WWW.JOSIEGOESGREEN.COM
TO SEND JOSIE A MESSAGE.

About Kenny Bruno

Kenny has worked in the environmental movement for over 25 years, on issues ranging from toxic waste in local communities to international negotiations in the UN system. He is co-author of:: Greenwash: The Reality Behind Corporate Environmentalism, and EarthSummit.Biz: The Corporate Takeover of Sustainable Development. Kenny is the founder of two schools for indigenous leaders on human rights and environment. Josie's "campaigns" are inspired by Kenny's experience as an environmental activist.

About Antonia Bruno

Antonia is a Political Science major at SUNY Binghamton. She has won awards from the Brooklyn Poet Laureate, the CUNY N.Y.C. Annual Poetry Festival and the Random House Writing Competition. In High School, Antonia wrote with Girls Write Now, A New York City-based organization that works with aspiring young women writers. She has been the President of her campus chapter of

DemocracyMatters. Antonia sets the tone of the Josie series and creates characters that elementary school kids can relate to.

About Beth Handman

Beth has been a teacher, educational consultant, curriculum specialist, staff developer and administrator for over 30 years. At her current school, P.S. 321, she collaborates closely with Teachers College Reading and Writing Project at Columbia University. Beth has been a Lucretia Crocker Fellow for the state of Massachusetts and has consulted extensively for New Visions for Public Schools. As a supervisor of literacy and curriculum, Beth guides the pedagogical aspects of the Josie series.

About Janet Pedersen

Janet Pedersen has illustrated many books for children, as well as authored a few herself. She is the author and illustrator of Houdini the Amazing Caterpillar (Clarion Books) and Millie in the Meadow (Candlewick Press). Janet lives with her family in Brooklyn, in a neighborhood a little like Josie's.

CPSIA information can be obtained at www.ICGtesting.com
Printed in the USA
LVOW11s0732170914

404483LV00002B/4/P